DATE DUE			
NOV 28 '02			
Lac			

626266 0159

Blizzards

By Duncan Scheff

Raintree Steck-Vaughn Publishers
A Harcourt Company

Austin · New York
www.steck-vaughn.com

Copyright © 2002, Steck-Vaughn Company

All rights reserved. No part of this book may be reproduced or utilized in any form or by any means, electronic or mechanical, including photocopying, recording, or by any information storage and retrieval system, without permission in writing from the publisher. Inquiries should be addressed to Copyright Permissions, Steck-Vaughn Company, P.O. Box 26015, Austin, TX 78755.

Published by Raintree Steck-Vaughn Publishers,
an imprint of Steck-Vaughn Company.

Library of Congress Cataloging-in-Publication Data

Blizzards/by Duncan Scheff.
p.cm.—(Nature on the rampage)
Includes bibliographical references and index.
ISBN 0-7398-4701-5
1. Blizzards—Juvenile literature. [1. Blizzards.] I. Title. II. Series.
QC926.37 .S32 2001
551.55'5—dc21

2001019823

Printed and bound in the United States of America
1 2 3 4 5 6 7 8 9 10 WZ 05 04 03 02 01

Produced by Compass Books

Photo Acknowledgments
Corbis/Bettmann, 20
Digital Stock, cover, 26
Michael Friang, 10, 14
Mike Jones, title page
Photodisk, 29
Photo Network/Brooks Dodge, 7; Jim Church, 18; Mark Sherman, 24
Root Resources/John Kahout, 4, 23

Content Consultants
Dr. Len Keshishian
State University of New York
Department of Earth Sciences

Maria Kent Rowell
Science Consultant
Sebastopol, California

David Larwa
National Science Education Consultant
Educational Training Services
Brighton, Michigan

This book supports the National Science Standards.

Contents

What Are Blizzards? 5

All About Blizzards 11

Blizzards in History 19

Science and Blizzards 27

Glossary 30

Internet Sites and Addresses 31

Index 32

Blizzards usually strike cold, northern climates.

What Are Blizzards?

A blizzard is a powerful winter storm with snow and strong winds. Blizzards can be small or large. Some blizzards cover many states at once. Others may happen only over one place. Blizzards can last from a few hours to several days.

Blizzards occur in many parts of the world. In North America, they are common in the northern part of the United States and all of Canada. They sometimes happen in southern states as well.

About three to five blizzards strike the United States each year. Most blizzards form in the months of December, January, and February.

When the Snow Flies

Blizzards can be killer storms. Heavy snow can break tree branches or make roofs fall. Blowing snow decreases **visibility** while driving or walking. During blizzards, many people are in danger of dying from cold or from car accidents.

Strong blizzard winds whip snow around until it creates a whiteout. A whiteout is a condition that makes it very hard to see things in the distance, even a few feet away. The snow hides objects from view and makes everything look white. People can easily get lost during a whiteout. Drivers may not be able to see the road and may drive their cars into ditches.

Blizzard winds also push snow into huge piles called drifts. The drifts block sidewalks, doors, and streets. Some drifts are so high that they bury people's houses or cars.

Blizzard winds also knock down trees, power lines, and telephone lines. People may lose electricity and heat in their homes. They

▲ **This snowplow is clearing snow off a road so that people can drive safely.**

may not be able to reach other people by phone if they need help.

During winter storms, it is best to stay safe indoors. During blizzards, snowplows cannot remove snow quickly enough to make driving safe. Snowplows are special trucks made for shoveling snow from roads.

Windchill Chart

THERMOMETER READING
(in Fahrenheit)

WIND SPEED (mph)	40°	30°	20°	10°	0°	-10°	-20°	-30°
Calm	40°	30°	20°	10°	0°	-10°	-20°	-36°
5	37°	27°	16°	6°	-5°	-15°	-26°	-58°
10	28°	16°	4°	-9°	-24°	-33°	-46°	-72°
20	18°	4°	-10°	-25°	-39°	-53°	-67°	-88°
30	13°	-2°	-18°	-33°	-48°	-63°	-79°	-97°
40	10°	-6°	-21°	-37°	-53°	-69°	-86°	-102°

This chart shows how temperature and wind speed affects the windchill factor. To use the chart, find the temperature in the top column of the chart. Then look at the wind speed in the left column. Follow the row leading across from wind speed and the column leading down from the temperature. The windchill factor is the point where they meet.

Windchills, Frostbite, and Hypothermia

People without shelter are in the greatest danger during blizzards. Blowing wind often makes the temperature seem colder. Low temperatures and winds create very cold windchills. A windchill is how cold the air feels on your skin when the wind is blowing. Wind blows heat away from your body, causing you to feel much colder.

Low windchills can hurt or kill people. To keep safe, people should cover all of their skin with warm clothes, boots, gloves, hats, and scarves. They should stay outside for only a short amount of time.

Uncovered skin is in danger of **frostbite**. Frostbite occurs when skin freezes. Areas of white or red will appear on skin with frostbite. In cases of bad frostbite, body parts, such as fingers, toes, and ears, may fall off or have to be cut off by doctors.

Hypothermia is dangerous too. It occurs when the body temperature falls too far below normal. With hypothermia, a person's heart beats slower. A person's blood flows away from arms and legs and into the body's main organs. Because of the blood flow, muscles do not work well. A person may feel sleepy and confused. If they do not get help, people with hypothermia can freeze to death.

People should wear coats, hats, and gloves to keep warm during blizzards.

All About Blizzards

Scientists place winter storms into several groups. Snowstorms include heavy snowfall. Ice storms include rain that turns into ice when it hits the cold ground. Cold and windchill **advisories** are given when temperatures are very low.

All blizzards have things in common. To be a blizzard, storms must have winds of at least 35 miles (56 km) per hour. This wind must blow snow, making it hard to see more than one-fourth of a mile (0.4 km) in front of you. The temperature must be below 20° Fahrenheit (-6° C). These conditions must take place for three hours before a storm can be called a blizzard.

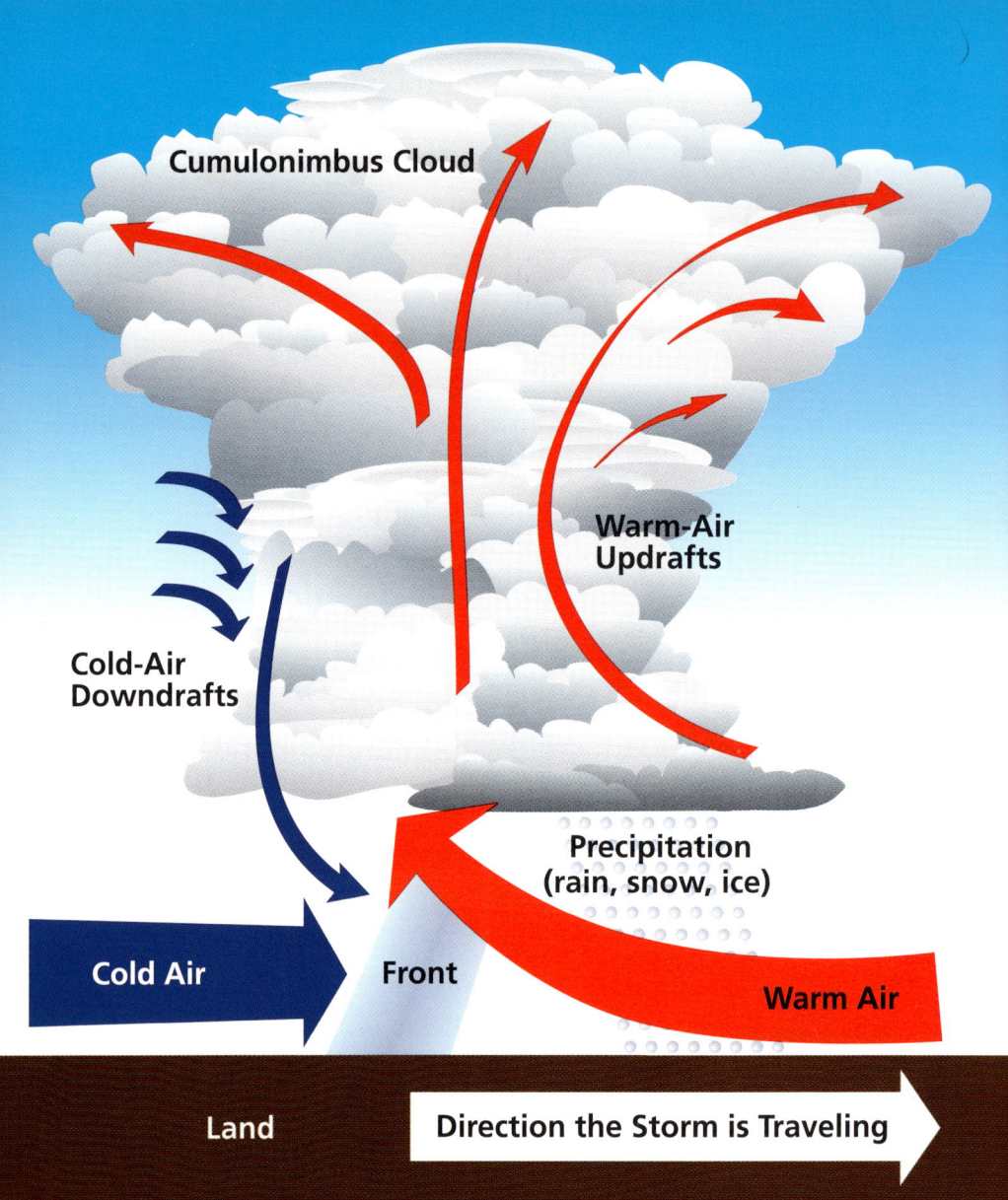

This illustration shows how a blizzard forms.

How Blizzards Form

Almost all storms happen when large masses of air meet. The edges of these masses of air are called **fronts**. A front has air that is about the same temperature and contains the same amount of moisture, or water. Blizzards sometimes strike when a winter storm moves into a place with a very cold temperature.

Warm air holds more moisture than cold air. Warm air also weighs less than cold air does. When warm and cold air meet, the warm air rises over the cold air. The warm air cools as it rises. The cooling air can no longer hold all of its moisture. During a blizzard, this moisture turns into snow.

Wind forms when two air masses meet. The wind can become strong if the air masses have very different temperatures. During a blizzard, the two air masses usually have a large difference in temperature. As the warm air rises, cool air rushes in to take its place. This causes the strong winds.

▲ **A nor'easter dumped so much snow on New York City that it buried cars, such as this one.**

Kinds of Blizzards

Several kinds of blizzards are common in North America. One kind is the nor'easter. During this storm, warm moist air from the south moves north up the eastern coast. This warm air meets cold air from eastern Canada and the North Atlantic. Soon the wind blows stronger, and snow starts to fall. Strong northeast winds from the northern Atlantic Ocean bring heavy snow and high winds as they blow onto the coast.

Alberta Clippers begin near the Rocky Mountains in Alberta, Canada. These blizzards are usually strong, but short. Alberta Clippers usually move southeast toward Manitoba, Canada. They often reach places in the northern United States. In Texas, strong winds from the North are called Northers.

Lake-effect blizzards take place near large bodies of water, such as the Great Lakes. Most of these lakes do not completely freeze during winter. The water temperature is often much higher than the air temperature. Some of the water evaporates into the warm air. Evaporate means that it turns into a gas. The lowest layer of air warms slightly as it passes over the land. It rises and meets the cooler air above. The water vapor cools as it rises and water droplets form. These droplets turn to snow or ice as they fall through the cooler air.

Beaufort Scale

Beaufort Number	Type of Gale	Wind Speed mph	Wind Speed km/h	Conditions
7	Moderate	32-38	51-61	Large branches in motion; whistling in telephone wires
8	Fresh	39-46	62-74	Twigs break off trees
9	Strong	47-54	75-87	Larger branches break off; some damage to buildings
10	Whole	55-63	88-101	Seldom experienced inland; trees uprooted; much damage to buildings

▲ **This chart shows the part of the Beaufort Wind Scale that measures gales.**

What Is a Gale?

High winds set blizzards apart from other winter storms. Blizzards usually include **gale**-force winds. A gale is a wind that blows from 32 to 63 miles (51 to 101 km) per hour.

Scientists measure wind force on the Beaufort Wind Scale. Sir Francis Beaufort developed this scale in 1805. Winds are measured with a Beaufort number based on their force. A Beaufort number of zero means there is no wind. The highest Beaufort number is 12.

The Beaufort Wind Scale separates gales into four groups. Their Beaufort numbers are seven through 10. Moderate gales are from 32 to 38 miles (51 to 61 km) per hour. Fresh gales are from 39 to 46 miles (62 to 74 km) per hour. Strong gales are from 47 to 54 miles (75 to 87 km) per hour. Whole gales are from 55 to 63 miles (88 to 101 km) per hour.

Moderate gales and fresh gales are most common during blizzards. These winds can break small limbs from trees.

Strong gales and whole gales can also occur. These winds can destroy buildings and trees.

Blizzards today are as strong and powerful as those in the past. A blizzard has buried this house. People have dug out the door so they can get in and out.

Blizzards in History

Throughout history, blizzards have been a problem for people who live in cold, snowy climates. A climate is the usual weather of a place.

The word "blizzard" came from German settlers in Iowa. They called the storms "blitzartig," which means "lightning-like." The German settlers were surprised at the strength of winter storms in North America.

People began to study and understand weather patterns in the 1800s. A pattern is something that repeats. Still, people at this time had no way to to send warnings. People had to carefully watch the weather on their own.

▲ These workers are removing snow that fell in New York during the Blizzard of 1888.

The Blizzard of 1888

One of the first blizzards to be recorded happened in 1888. This was a powerful nor'easter named the Blizzard of 1888.

The Blizzard of 1888 began as a rainstorm. But temperatures quickly dropped as a cold front collided with warm air. Cold winds from the north grew stronger, and the rain turned to snow.

    The storm lasted for more than a day. It hit places from Maine to Washington, D.C. Parts of Massachusetts and New York received up to 50 inches (127 cm) of snow. Other states along the East Coast also received a great deal of snow. About 400 people died because of the blizzard.

    The Blizzard of 1888 caused cities to change the way they handle winter storms. Cars, trains, and roads in New York were buried in snow. Houses in the country were buried too. Some people were trapped for several days. They had to dig tunnels through the snow. Because of these problems, some cities began searching for ways to remove snow from roadways. Other cities built subway trains that could run underground during winter storms.

Later Blizzards

One of the worst blizzards on record was the Armistice Day Blizzard of 1940. This blizzard occurred across the upper Midwest on November 11.

The day began warm. Temperatures were as high as 60 degrees in the late morning and early afternoon. Then the temperatures quickly dropped. Snow began to fall, and the wind became strong. Many people were caught in the blizzard without winter clothing. The blizzard lasted for more than two days. More than 150 people died.

Another famous blizzard occurred in March of 1993 along the East Coast. This blizzard was called the Storm of the Century. The blizzard stretched from Georgia to Canada. It lasted almost three days. It dropped snow on the whole eastern half of the United States. Airports and highways along the East Coast closed. Millions of people went days without electricity. More than 200 people died in the storm.

This woman is shoveling snow that fell during the Storm of the Century.

▲ People in this town are being safe by staying inside during the blizzard.

How Can People Survive Blizzards?

There are things people can do to stay safer during blizzards. First, they should not try to travel during a winter storm. Roads can become slippery or hidden by snow. Strong winds can blow small cars off the road.

 Did you know that a snowflake is made of tiny ice crystals that have frozen together? Snowflakes have some things in common. They each have six sides. They form three general shapes—ice plates, needles, or columns. Even so, there are so many different shapes and sizes of snowflakes that some people say that no two snowflakes are exactly alike!

People may also get stuck on a road for a long time without any help.

People who must travel during a winter storm should be very careful. They should carry a survival kit in their cars. A survival kit should include first-aid supplies, warm blankets, food, and water. A kit also may include matches, a candle, a flashlight, and a bright piece of cloth to use as a signal in case a person needs rescue.

People who are caught outdoors during a blizzard should try to find shelter. This keeps them safe from the winds.

This meteorologist is gathering information to see what the weather will be like.

SCIENCE AND BLIZZARDS

Scientists who study the weather are called **meteorologists**. Some of these scientists study blizzards. They search for the causes of blizzards. Meteorologists hope to save lives by giving people early warnings about blizzards that are coming.

Meteorologists give watches or warnings over TV and radio when there is danger of a blizzard. A winter storm watch means heavy snow and ice may fall within 48 hours. A blizzard warning means that heavy snow and high winds will strike within 24 hours. A severe blizzard warning means that heavy snow and winds of more than 45 miles (72 km) per hour will strike within 24 hours.

Scientific Tools

Meteorologists use many different tools to help them track and **predict** weather patterns. Predict is to make an educated guess about the future. **Satellites** are spacecraft in orbit that send information back to Earth. Weather satellites send meteorologists pictures of cloud patterns. The meteorologists use satellite pictures to identify fronts, air masses, thunderstorms, and blizzards.

Meteorologists sometimes use Doppler radar to study weather patterns, too. This instrument uses radio waves to help scientists learn about clouds and thunderstorms. It tells them about the strength of a thunderstorm and the speed it is moving.

Meteorologists use the information they learn to form weather forecasts. A weather forecast predicts what future weather will be.

The Future

Meteorologists today still have trouble predicting the weather. Every year, they learn more about what causes certain kinds of

▲ **This weather satellite is taking pictures of clouds as it orbits Earth.**

weather. Improvements to computers, satellites, and Doppler radar also help.

Scientists hope that better machines and more information will help them to predict the weather better. By giving people warnings on time, scientists hope to save lives.

Glossary

advisory (ad-VIZE-oh-ree)—information given about possibly dangerous weather conditions

front (FRUHNT)—the edge of a large air mass where it meets another air mass

frostbite (FRAWST-bite)—a condition that occurs when cold air freezes skin

gale (GALE)—a wind that blows from 32 to 63 miles (51 to 101 km) per hour

hypothermia (hye-puh-THUR-mee-uh)—a condition in which a person's body temperature drops far below normal

meteorologist (mee-tee-ur-OL-oh-jist)—a scientist who studies weather

predict (pri-DIKT)—to make an educated guess about a future event

satellite (SAT-uh-lite)—a spacecraft that orbits Earth

visibility (viz-uh-BIL-uh-tee)—the distance an average person can see outdoors

Internet Sites and Addresses

National Weather Service
http://www.nws.noaa.gov/

Storm Encyclopedia: Winter Storms
http://www.weather.com/encyclopedia/winter/
   index.html

University of Illinois—Snow
http://ww2010.atmos.uiuc.edu/(Gh)/guides/
   mtr/cld/prcp/snow.rxml

The Weather Dude
http://www.wxdude.com/

American Meteorological Society
45 Beacon Street
Boston, MA 02108-3693

National Weather Service
1324 East-West Highway
Silver Spring, MD 20910

INDEX

advisories, 11
Alberta Clippers, 15

Beaufort Wind Scale, 16-17
Blizzard of 1888, 20-21

forecast, 28
front, 13, 21, 28
frostbite, 8, 9

gale, 16

hypothermia, 8, 9

ice storm, 11

lake-effect blizzards, 15

nor'easter, 14
Northers, 15

satellite, 28
snowplows, 7
Storm of the Century, 22
survival kit, 25

warning, 27
watch, 27